The UGLY DUCKLING
and other
CLASSIC FAIRY TALES

D1386294

igloobooks

The Ugly Duckling

Once, near a little farm, on a riverbank,
a duck sat on her nest of eggs. Suddenly, the eggs began
to **CRACK** and tiny heads poked out.

Quack, quack went the little ducklings.

However, one duckling didn't look like the others.
It was large, grey and ugly. "I shall take it to the river
and see if it can swim like my other babies,"
said the mother duck.

The ducklings jumped in the water...

... Splash!

"The grey one swims just like the others," said the mother duck. She decided that the ducklings should meet the animals on the little farm, nearby.

In the farmyard, the animals looked at
the new arrivals. They thought the grey duckling
was **very** ugly. The poor duckling was bullied,
even by his brothers and sisters.

"You're SO ugly," they cried.
The ugly duckling ran away to hide
in the reeds of the marsh.

Woof, woof!

Two fierce dogs ran past the ugly duckling, but they
didn't pay him any attention. **"Even they think I'm ugly,"**
said the duckling. So, he decided to leave the marsh.
After a while, he came to a cottage.

The old woman in the cottage let the duckling stay. The cat and hen who lived there said the little duckling should **purr** and **cluck** like them.

The duckling didn't want to **purr** or **cluck**. He wanted to swim. So, before long, he left the cottage.

Soon, winter arrived and the river
and reeds **froze**, trapping the little duckling
in the ice. Luckily, a kind man passed by.

He rescued the **shivering** duckling from
the ice and took him home.

The man's children were very excited and chased the duckling around the house.

"STOP!" screeched the man's wife, as the duckling upset the milk bucket.

He was so frightened, he ran outside into the falling snow.

Time passed and the duckling was alone through the **cold** winter. Then, spring came...

He **flapped** his wings and suddenly **soared** into the air.

Far below, the duckling saw three beautiful birds. "I shall fly to them," he said, "**even if they bully and tease me.**"

The birds did not tease the duckling.
"**Look at your reflection**," they said. The duckling
looked down at the water. No longer was he ugly,
but instead he was a **beautiful** swan.

At last, he had found where he belonged.

The Frog Prince

Once, a princess dropped her golden ball
in the royal pond. She was **VERY** upset.
"I'll get your ball," said a frog, who was sitting on a
lily pad. **"If I do though, you must let me...**

...**eat** off your plate,

drink from your cup,

and **sleep** in your bed."

"I promise," said the princess.

So, the frog got the ball. However, as soon
as he'd brought it to the surface, the princess
grabbed it and ran away.

The next day, the frog visited the princess.

"Ugh, it's **you!"**
the princess cried.

"What's the matter?"
asked the king.

"I made a promise to this... thing," she explained.

"Then you must keep it," demanded the king. So, the frog ate from the princess' plate and drank from her cup.

The frog gave a big **YAWN**.

"**I wish to sleep in your bedchamber,**" he said.

The princess looked horrified.

"**Never!**" she cried.

"**You will do as the frog asks,**" commanded the king.

With that, the frog slept in her bedchamber until dawn.

As the princess awoke, the frog spoke. "Kiss me and I promise I shall leave you alone forever."

The princess knew the frog would keep his promise,
so she closed her eyes and **kissed** him.
"Yuck!" she said.

The princess opened her eyes and standing in front of her was a **handsome**, young man.

"I'm a prince," he said.

"I was **cursed** and your kiss set me free."

So, the princess and the prince fell in love, and they lived

happily ever after.

Puss in Boots

Once, a poor miller gave each of his three sons a gift.
All he had left for his youngest son was a cat.
The son was very disappointed until he realised
the cat could **speak**.

"Give me a pair of boots and I'll make you a **prince**," it said.

With nothing to lose,
the son **agreed**.

The clever cat brought juicy rabbits to the king, who was very impressed.

"Who is your master?" asked the king.

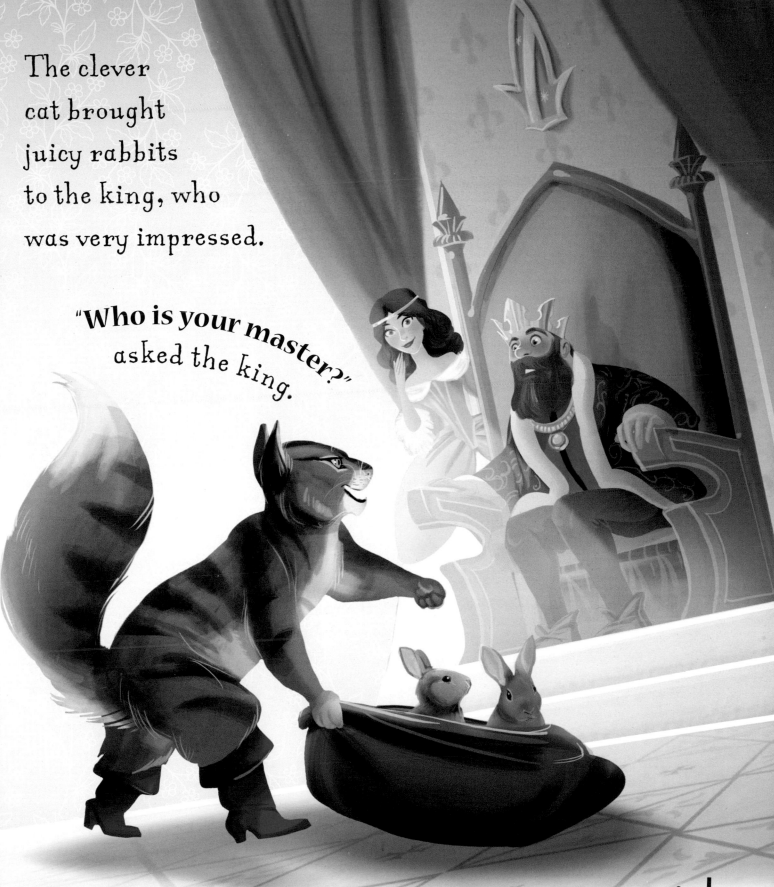

The cat wanted to make the miller's son sound **special**, so he replied, **"The Marquis of Carabas."**

"I want the Marquis to **marry** my daughter," said the king. "In fact, I'll visit him now."

The **cunning** cat rushed home, asked his master to undress and stand in the river. Soon, the king arrived. "Help!" cried the cat. "**The Marquis has been robbed.**"

The king dressed the son in **fine** clothes
and sat him next to the princess.

They instantly fell in **love**.

Meanwhile, the cat spoke to some farm workers.
**"Tell the king this land belongs to the Marquis of
Carabas, or he'll be very angry,"** he said.

Next, the cat visited a castle where a **FIERCE** ogre, who could change shape, lived.
"Can you really change shape?" asked the cat.

"Of course," replied the ogre, who became a lion.

"A mouse?" asked the cat.

"Easy," replied the ogre.

With that, he transformed and the cat **gobbled** him up.

The king arrived at the castle. Believing it belonged to the miller's son, he immediately offered him his daughter's hand in **marriage**.

So it was that the young man became a prince and they all lived

happily ever after.